In the new house, we have two human house-mates. A brunette woman and a blond male. I wear a wig. Otherwise I look perfectly human. But around the housemates, my boyfriend acts differently toward me. He tells them, "We're just friends."

— "I Will Work for Love," by Heather Sager

Star Crossed

Vol. 1

New Tales of Strange Love, Weird Romance Polymorphic Passion, & Feverish Fabulism

From the Editors of The Fabulist

Contents

About the Stories

This is not a romance anthology.

To be sure, this book is overbrimming with love, passion, yearning, attachment, need, fulfillment, obsession, and frustration! Yet there are, this time around (it is, after all, intended to be merely the first volume in a series), no bodices ripped.

And the endings, even if they are happy, tend to be … complicated. All the magic, mystery, alienating technologies, warped realities and strange transformations contained within these pages are, in their distortions of the ordinary, a means of clarifying our shared condition as fundamentally emotional, romantic creatures. The funhouse mirror of fantastical literature captures hidden contours of the heart. The fantasies we share reveal true things:

Emotional turmoil is externalized in startling, spectacular, and even shocking physiological displays.

The social construct of *relationships* transforms the body, and occludes the self ...

Love is literally explosive, and love pulls the hot mess back together again.

Time travel! What would you change? Or would you merely act out your unhealthy obsessions, again and again and again?

Virtual reality ... an idealized mirror to our imperfect world—or a quagmire of simulation, simulacra, delusion, and disassociation?

There are angels in these pages, and everything that makes them different makes them so very, very human ...

Our "star crossed" lovers are not meant to find fulfillment; unknowable forces from the depths of the psyche block their communion, and the tiniest moments of togetherness are great victories. When we invert the cliches of genre fiction, we are marvelously liberated.

This is not a romance anthology. It is a map made of words, leading us, by various winding paths, deep into the heart of the matter. The journey is, of course, the destination ...

—San Francisco, March 2025

Reptilia

By Ruth Crossman

HER TONGUE hasn't always been this way. She's pretty sure it was round and pink and human-like when she was born. It's taken a steady diet of coffee and swear words to get her to this point, but now it's unavoidable.

The fork began with one word said in a fit of anger: something acid and venomous that made him recoil. She saw the look in his eyes—something between anger and fear, and when she opened her mouth again to apologize only hissing came out.

She tries to compensate for it, keeping her mouth shut tight and ladylike, but she can't pull it off. It's starting to change the way she says words. Now everything comes out sibilant—even when she's just ordering coffee or trying to make small talk with the cashier at the corner store.

Her throat is beginning to close up and throb. When she feels something bitter welling up like milk she realizes the venom gland is kicking in.

She worries about the effect it will have on him—is it safe to kiss open-mouthed? She's sure the fangs can't be far behind now, but he just looks sad.

It's okay. Her eyes are closed and he strokes the new scales on her hands. *It's okay, really.*

I Will Work for Love
By Heather Sager

TALL HOUSES scrape at the blue, white-cloudy sky. The neighborhood grass glows green. This doesn't look at all like the cyborg farm.

My boyfriend is driving. I sit in the backseat with the laundry. I wear human clothes, just like him, and I sort our wearables as we rush onward.

I also glance out at the many doors, facades, and driveways of our new neighborhood. The houses look the same, except varying in their pastel colorings and differing slightly in height.

We arrive at our new house.

My greatest hope is that my boyfriend, who of course is a human, will select me for marriage. He says he might, because I have a Protestant work ethic. I once asked what that meant. We women from the cyborg farm do not know about Protestants or other religious sects.

"It just means you work hard," he had replied. I still want to know more, for I find philosophies fascinating.

We unpack and settle in and I hope he will tell me. But whenever I allow my recursive brain structures to ponder and explore, and state aloud my queries, he turns on the television.

I used to write poetry at the cyborg farm. One of my poems went like this: *I may be more than half robot, but I have a heart and feel love.* When my boyfriend purchased me, he told the owner of the cyborg farm that time is money. I didn't ask what that meant; I still don't want to know.

In the new house, we have two human housemates. A brunette woman and a blond male. I wear a wig. Otherwise I look perfectly human. But around the housemates, my boyfriend acts differently toward me. He tells them, "We're just friends."

But that's not true. We sleep together most nights, except the nights he rejects me. Then I shiver and cry in my own room, on a narrow bed. I don't like that room, because there are no lights and it's very dark. There are no decorations, but I'd like to add some for the nights I have to spend there.

Watching the three humans play out in the green yard on weekends, I feel my dreams slipping away. I press my face against the window's cool pane of glass.

My boyfriend doesn't like it here. He calls it "suburban hell." But I like the yards with their children, dogs, and sprinklers. It's much nicer than the cyborg farm, stuffed with straw and machinery and factory belts. Perhaps happiness is a façade, like the one a house has, I tell myself. Once you get past the front of happiness, there is quiet and sadness and doubt.

I drive to a large building and work there on weekdays. There are engineers, and marketing and science personnel. My boss is a round-faced, complacent man. He meets me daily in the front lobby, and takes me to my office. "Processor Drone One, it's good to meet you," he says to me each time, as if I've forgotten. I follow him upstairs and get plugged in to my networking port. I don't have time to write poetry anymore, not like at the cyborg farm.

"You might have noticed half your paycheck is missing," my boss told me at the end of the first month. "It's because we paid that half to Mr. Billingsley."

Mr. Billingsley is what the world calls my boyfriend. I still work even though my boyfriend gets half my check. I guess this is why he likes my Protestant work ethic. Out of all my tasks at the office, I enjoy writing instruction manuals because I feel the work is more human than machine. Also, when I work on them, I get to sit and look out the swrindows at the small and tender trees that encircle the building.

In the spring, we attend a wedding. My

boyfriend tells me he thinks the ceremony is a rather dull proceeding. But I find the exchange of vows and overall atmosphere painfully exquisite. I hold back tears.

That night, when he reaches for me in bed, I feel a supreme melancholy. I think: *I will never be his wife.*

The next week, I get a raise! I feel like flying and don't know what's next. The sky seems forever blue when I walk on my lunch break. When I go home and tell my boyfriend, he says that he can afford to kick out the housemates, which he then does. "Now there's no need to pretend between us," he says. I am glowing. I am really, really hoping for things to be different.

"I am happy to be a good citizen," I tell my boyfriend. I trim the trees in the backyard. I cook dinners. He is so tall and handsome, my boyfriend. When he holds me, and I listen for his heartbeat, I feel I can move mountains. I think, one day soon, he might give me an engagement ring. Then I will feel the sort of happiness I only imagine in dreams.

Late on a Sunday, we are resting up. "I want to go to school, to a real university," I tell him.

"Why?" he says.

"I can work better if I learn more," I reply.

He frowns. "True, but the university is very expensive."

"You're right," I sigh, and am filled with sadness.

Then he leads me up to his closet. He opens

it. "Look," he says. Books clutter the closet—many of them. "These are my books from engineering school. You can learn all you want," he says. I jump for happiness.

He watches TV a lot. I listen to Brahms and Bach and Hank Williams, trying to understand emotions. Emotions are a curious thing. Do I feel music? When I play music, when my boyfriend is turned away from me and watching television, I feel disturbed by unknown vibrations in my soul.

"I want for us to get married," I tell my boyfriend one day. "Because I like to feel as if I am moving forward, and that makes me feel powerful. If we were married, I would feel as if our love is moving forward too. Perhaps I can even get another work promotion, because I am so happy."

I don't think too much when I say this. But, after those last words emerge from my mouth, he gives me the most curious, sly smile.

A week later, an engagement ring appears. Six months later, we get married. It's a civic ceremony, so I never meet his relatives. But I feel, at last, content. My new husband is the world to me.

Our marriage wears on. Something strange happens to me. I start to forget about my husband a little and start noticing other people again, even more than I used to. I notice the poetry in the lives of people in my busy neighborhood. The elderly Indian couple who hold hands as they walk. The teenage girl who reclines under the weeping willow with her book. Children playing at the park. They shine in their beauty.

I go out to simply watch. I can't have children of my own. Now that my situation is stable, and I do not have to be returned to the cyborg farm, watching the children and other people is a relief to me.

Once a cyborg is married off, she's hardly ever returned. Hardly.

♥

The Incredible Exploding Woman

By Jamie Hittman

WALT RETURNED from work to find that his wife had exploded in the middle of the living room. At ground zero was a great bloody starburst, and at its center were Molly's slippered feet, blown off at the ankles. All around her, the walls and furniture were lashed with long tongues of gore.

Walt ran from the room, and fell back against the wall of the foyer, groaning, scrubbing his face with his hands.

Before they got married, the couples' counselor had warned them that while Molly was improving, relapses could still happen. Recovery was a process, not an endpoint.

"Remember that Molly has a *condition*," she told Walt. "If she has a setback, you must be there for her."

Walt made himself return to the living room. Blood spattered the sofa, the windows, and the bassinet where their child lay crying. Next to Molly's severed feet was the vacuum cleaner, still switched on.

How much of this was his fault? Walt wondered. That morning, they had gotten into a shouting match, because he had scolded Molly for working too hard, for not knowing how to ask for help.

"I'm fine," Molly had said, as she always said, especially when it wasn't true. "I'm fine."

Walt unplugged the vacuum, rocked their baby back to sleep, then slunk out to the garage to get his gear.

The counselor had advised against wearing too much PPE, stating that excessive barriers would impede the healing process, but Walt still wasn't ready to bloody his hands. He pulled on his galoshes and a pair of long rubber gloves and gathered his tools: a large metal bucket, a tote bag, an extendable squeegee, a hook on a pole, and a clawed trash picker with a trigger on the grip.

He squeegeed the blood off the walls and into his bucket, then used his trash picker to grab his wife's feet. He found several bones knocking wetly against each another, trying and failing to put themselves back together. Walt placed them in his bucket as well.

Next, he found the hollow wetsuit of Molly's skin draped across the back of the couch, and then, to his great relief, he found her head, which had landed atop the snake plant in the corner. Molly's eyes were closed, and she appeared to be peacefully sleeping. Walt stowed her head at the bottom of his tote bag.

That's when he noticed her right hand next to the planter, clenched around her cell phone. Walt heard a woman's voice still yammering from the speaker. The caller ID read: "MOM (THAT BITCH)."

Molly was an only child. Her father had died suddenly years ago, which left Molly as her mother's sole emotional support. Her mother would call her day and night, and Walt was witness to many one-sided conversations, hours in length, where Molly played the perfect daughter, endlessly placating.

Yes, mother. No, mother. Of course, mother.

One night, after an argument about the wedding guest list, Molly had blown up beneath the covers of their bed. It had taken both Walt and Molly days to steam clean the bedroom and replace the bloodied sheets, and Walt was terrified that the next explosion would be at the ceremony.

Every day, Molly would repeat a mantra: *I will not go to pieces. I will not go to pieces.*

She even had the phrase written on their cake, which she had commissioned from a bakery specializing in hyper-realistic desserts.

On their wedding day, Molly ignored her mother, exchanged her vows with Walt, and then the two of them cut the cake. The outside of the cake was white buttercream frosting—but the inside was a garish, fleshy red, shot through with white marbling, like a side of raw meat. A dark red cherry sauce oozed out as the knife sank in. Molly's mother observed the scene in horrified bemusement. Molly just smiled and smushed the cake slice into Walt's face.

"I wanted to remind her that I'm flesh and blood, too," Molly said later.

Walt didn't need any such reminders. He found Molly's liver attempting to disguise itself as a cushion on the loveseat, while her heart tried to stage a get-away, using her lungs as wet wings.

Her large intestine had looped itself about the blades of the ceiling fan—like a sleeping cobra; Walt lifted it free with his hook.

Satisfied, Walt stowed his tools and carried the bucket upstairs to the bathroom. The rest of Molly's parts would come back on their own.

Here, he poured the blood and guts in the tub and stared at the mess, dreading what he now had to do. How easy it was to forget the parts that made up a person—the vulnerable innards, curled away from the world's sharp edges, from the knives of expectation, from all those inter-personal barbs designed to hurt.

He undressed and climbed into the tub.

Molly's blood was still warm, vital enough to be returned to its source. Walt leaned against the back of the tub.

"I love you, Molly," he said. "I love you."

The blood rippled gently as Molly began to reassemble herself. Her organs climbed back inside her skin, which zipped itself closed around them. Her remaining bones clattered in through the doorway and jammed themselves into her arms and legs. Molly's hands lifted her head and placed it atop the stump of her head with a lightbulb twist, and then Molly opened her eyes, shivering.

"Walt?" she asked. Her eyes roved his blood-spattered nakedness. "It happened again, didn't it?"

Walt studied the face of the woman he loved. Sweet, beautiful Molly. She hadn't healed, not yet. But she was trying. She was whole. He wrapped his arms around her and she wrapped her arms around him. There would be time enough later to clean up the mess. For now, they just held on and listened to each other breathe.

Gustavo and Emiline

By Elizabeth Stix

GUSTAVO CAME to Emiline from above. He was round as a hot air balloon but heavy as a walrus, with little flipper feet and pudgy hands flapping out from his sides. He descended upon her from the sky, darkening out the daylight above her, waving his stubby arms and feet as his balloon-body glided earthward, until he alit, square on top of her, and let out a satisfied sigh of relief.

"Oh," Emiline cried. He sat on her back, squashing her face into the sidewalk. The pavement scratched at her and a pebble dug into her cheek. "Get up, Gustavo!" she wailed. "You're crushing me! I can't breathe!"

Gustavo rolled around on top of her, reveling in the softness of his landing. Emiline dragged her fingernails along the pavement and kicked her feet in the air, but if he knew that he had landed on her, Gustavo did not care.

Emiline married Gustavo because she loved him like a brother, the brother she had always longed for when she was a girl. She had grown up by herself, an only child to parents who worked at the university laboratory and came home and buried themselves under the papers on their desks, piled as high as haystacks. Emiline would knock on their study door. She could hear the papers rustle.

"Come in!" her mother would cry. Emiline would peer around the heavy oaken door. She'd see a hand clutching eyeglasses sticking out amid the heap of manuscripts and data tables, or perhaps she would find her father's shoe, kicked off and thrown across the room.

"Do I disturb you?" Emiline would ask.

"Of course not, dear," her mother would answer. "Did you finish your dinner?"

"Yes," Emiline would lie. She hadn't finished her dinner. She'd fed it to her imaginary brother and saved the cold bits for herself.

"Hand me my cup of tea, would you, darling?"

Emiline would push the teacup and saucer closer to the large pile, while her mother's delicate hand waved blindly.

"Thank you, dear," said her mother, curling a long finger around the teacup's ear-shaped grasp.

Emiline withdrew to bed.

When Emiline met Gustavo, he was the first

person who had ever listened to her. He used to tell her, "I want to know everything about you. Are you hot, are you cold? I want to know. Are you frightened? What did you have for breakfast?"

"I had oatmeal, with almonds and sunflower seeds," Emiline would tell him.

"Sunflower seeds!" Gustavo would proclaim. "My sunflower. You shine with a brilliance few women will ever know."

There was more. He liked to brush Emiline's hair, plucking out the burrs and stickums that had landed there during the day, working out the knots with warm oil. His hands were strong, and sometimes he would stroke his thumbs along the nape of her neck until she felt herself surrender.

He had a big walnut bed with a patchwork quilt and flannel sheets, and Emiline liked to burrow herself there, watching the dust motes dance in a strip of morning light that cut through the room and landed in a shiny pool on Emiline's jacket, which she sometimes dropped on the floor.

They had a small wedding in the back room of the courthouse. Gustavo's large family, whom Emiline had never met before and hadn't seen since, spilled out into the aisles and jostled each other for the best view of the bride and groom, taking photographs and murmuring with approval to each other as Gustavo and Emiline exchanged vows.

For fourteen months, Emiline was content. Gustavo brought her flowers on Friday afternoons, usually posies and snapdragons but sometimes yellow daisies. Emiline made shepherd's pie and goulash and casseroles that filled both of them up and usually put Gustavo to sleep, head on the table.

Shortly after their first anniversary, though, things began to change. First of all, Gustavo began to grow. Each breath he took sucked up more air. His hands became wider until his wedding ring would not come off, but gripped his finger like a tiny gold vise. When they went out to eat, Gustavo took up almost all of Emiline's field of vision as she sat opposite him at the table. Maybe it was the casseroles, or maybe it was some kind of an illusion, because he only seemed to grow large on certain days of the week. If Emiline looked at him suddenly, turned her head too quickly, he appeared bloated, puffy, his feet even floating a bit above the ground. If she turned her head slowly, and crept a glance at him quietly, there was Gustavo, back to his normal size, polishing the silverware and whistling a small tune.

Not long thereafter, Emiline began to feel as if she was being followed. Shadows in the alleyways reached out to her on the street, but she never found anyone there.

One day, instead of looking over her shoulder, Emiline looked up. And there he was. A dirigible in the sky. She squinted at him, covering her eyes from the bright sun, but she was certain of it. Gustavo floated high above her, coasting along in the summer breeze.

Day after day, it went on like this. In the grocery store, she'd feel his presence, and catch a glimpse of him hovering outside when she passed the window by the mangoes and kumquats. Gustavo trailed her on her errands, blotting out the sun, and when she stopped and had tea at a café, he shaded her newspaper and cooled the afternoon heat with his overbearing girth.

Some days, he would swoop down and land on her without warning, his shadow blossoming in size as he tumbled. She would try to run but he came too quickly and he would crush her, pinning her to the sidewalk, scraping her cheeks and giving her bruises on her arms and legs. The mangoes and kumquats would roll into the gutter.

No one seemed to notice, though a little dog tied to a post once barked wildly.

When she came home at night, he would be there, back to his normal size, whistling as he chopped the onions and poured the evening wine. She peered at him sideways, still tingling from the scratches and sidewalk burns.

He'd hand her a goblet of wine with a smile and a wink. Emiline looked at his hands, smooth and graceful, no longer bloated like water balloons. She drank her wine.

She vowed that she would talk to him about

it. But every time the moment seemed right, she would open her mouth, timidly, fish-like, and before she could speak, Gustavo would take up all the air. "You're my idol, baby," he would say. "Have I ever told you that? Every man on the street is jealous because I'm walking next to such a fine young thing. I dig that, Emiline. I dig you, and I dig that."

Gustavo stabbed radicchio and arugula drenched in olive oil and stuffed it in his mouth, salad dressing running down his chin in a rivulet that forked into a Y and then dripped onto the tablecloth.

Emiline's fish mouth closed. Opened. Closed.

Nighttimes were the worst. She would dream of her parents, now long dead, and her imaginary brother, long dead, too. How terribly she missed them. Emiline didn't want Gustavo's posies, or his snapdragons. She wanted to go home.

Emiline lay in bed, looking at the ceiling, and listened to Gustavo's heavy, labored breathing, remnants of the evening's goulash rattling around in his throat. She knew that in the morning the slice of light would cascade through the split in the curtains, decorating a shimmering wall between the window and the bed. She closed her eyes and looked forward to that.

Gustavo stirred. He clattered his throat and sniffled. He smacked his heavy lips. Emiline kept her eyes closed and imagined the golden wall of light, dancing for her in the morning.

The bed creaked and moaned and shifted, and Gustavo rolled his walrus body on top of her. Emiline opened her eyes and turned her head to the window, searching for a sign.

But Gustavo raised himself above her, and the moonlight disappeared.

Mystery of My Yearning for You, Winged One
By Patricia Flaherty Pagan

SWEETER THAN my daily duty of needlework and smiles is my hope that you, songbird paramour, will be mine. The lace embracing my boned collar is a noose, my suitors, execution-ers. The parlor stifles. Aunts hover. I must si-lence my tongue or catch the fever Henry James gave Daisy Miller.

Yet the mystery of my yearning for you, winged one, mischief-maker from a story I learned as a child, tugs at my skirt. If I speak golden words of love, will I wake to find you've come beyond the bars of your cage to me?

Through the French doors, the trees dip their

branches towards the lake in time with your chirp. Daydreams of your soft feathers against my fingertips fuel my strange ardor. Let your claws scratch my cheek: Is love in any form a truer melody than loneliness?

I must find the potion that will spark your transformation. Must know the weight of your man-body beside me. Feigning illness at tea time, I steal to the forest edge and buy herbs from the wise crone with black fingernails. Roots nip at my ankles and moss licks my shoes as I hurry home. Will the gardener discover my flight?

My parents and my priest would spurn me for my sins. Lust and bearing false witness. Neighbors would condemn me with gossip and the Book of Deuteronomy. But songbird, you've captured my soul.

Lining your cage with fennel, I recite Shelley poems like spells. Your lovely wings enchant. I peer into your small eyes, and desire stares back. Tonight, I will place an amber stone beneath my pillow, and lie down to dream.

♥

The Answerer
By Jenny Bitner

SHE WOKE with a feeling of fear in her whole body. It started in her belly and eased out in tentacles through her heart, her face, her throat, bathing her in a wash of anxiety, like Drano on her nerves. It stuck in her throat: a sentence that wanted to come but couldn't. And all of this because she couldn't make up her mind. How stupid. Why did anyone choose to tolerate this feeling? She had been up in the night going through the pros and cons of what to do, awash in this disgusting uncertainty.

That was it. This had to end.

She dialed the number from the ads. She let it ring. This time she didn't hang up. She heard the ringing like something very far away, an old phone that hung on the wall, black and heavy, like a hatchet. Where was the person answering the phone? Were they a person?

She remembered the first ad that she ever saw, years ago, that showed a wise old woman in the forest, a white woman with grey hair, a noble face, wearing robes, and the phone ringing (somehow in the middle of the forest) and the woman answering. Now the ads were more modern. They showed a person struggling with a problem and picking up the phone and dialing, and the voice on the other end was of unclear gender, unknown race, unknown age. The emphasis was on the person asking the question. They always looked so happy, so absolutely certain at the end of the call.

"Hello, how can I help you?" a voice said in the tone of someone who never gets angry, worries, or frets. She wanted to be that person. It sounded like a woman, but all the Answerers went by they.

"I have a problem ..."

Is it a problem? It's just indecision. It's normal.

"Of course you do," the soothing voice replied, a mountain lake.

"Can you help me?" Her voice was even, but in her head, she still heard her boyfriend's words: *Who would let a stranger make that kind of decision? It's such a weak move.*

She felt guilty just for making the call.

"Yes, of course I can," the voice replied, and she felt a quarter inch of space easing between the knife that she now realized she was holding to her own skin. The Drano feeling in her stomach eased a bit.

"I just don't know what to do," she said, "it's so complicated."

"Nothing is complicated, dear, we just make it so."

"Yes," she agreed. It was true, her terrible, cloudy mind was complicating things. "I think too much, and that's why I think you can help."

She noticed the word dear. It annoyed her slightly, but she had no idea how to parse it without knowing the gender, age, and ethnicity of the speaker, so she let it go.

"But of course. This is my job. I would love to help you."

She thought of the Answerer in their own life. how peaceful they must be. Always making the right decision without even having to ask for help.

She lay down on her bed again, atop the yellow duvet cover, where he had been yesterday. The color he said was as cheerful as a morning kiss. Yesterday, he had said that he loved being with her—but she had felt slightly bored. They had a weird conversation about oral sex. He wouldn't call it weird. He thought she overused that word. He had said he kinda liked oral sex, but it wasn't something he was that into. He did it for her, for her pleasure. She wondered why he was even bringing it up.

There are a lot of situations that fit the word "weird" for her. Weird is when your insides start to feel funny because the other person is saying something and in your mind, you start to see sheep jumping over a fence. She had been taught as a child to imagine sheep jumping to go to sleep, but it never felt right to her, and now she flashed on it from time to time when things were weird.

Once she asked her father what color the sheep were, and did they have shit stuck to their fur? He had looked at her like he didn't understand and said, "White, they are white. They're not real."

Why, she thought, would she imagine sheep that were not real when she could imagine real sheep? And what is the difference between an imagined imaginary sheep and an imagined real sheep? Weren't they all real in her imagination?

At the end of the conversation yesterday, she felt a little bad that her boyfriend was just licking her pussy because she liked it, while he was ambivalent and probably thinking about the chances of getting killed in a mass shooting when he went to the shopping mall. But then sometimes she felt like she was just doing everything in the whole relationship for him because he wanted something, and she didn't even know what she wanted.

Then the Answering Service had popped into her head. The service knew things. They had the best decisions. You didn't have to agonize over things for months or years or weeks. That was what they sold you on. Certainty.

"It's my boyfriend," she told the Answerer.

"Yes, so many times it is. How many are you paying for?"

"Just one, I think."

"OK, just be clear. Be sure. Sometimes people make a mistake and then they are overcharged."

"How does that happen?"

"It's the interrogatory nature of language. Sometimes people inadvertently ask questions. Like for example, 'Can you help?' If I were unscrupulous, the way some of us are, I could even count that."

"Count that?" Her stomach jumped. Was this Answerer trying to rip her off?

"Yes, it's an item. We charge by the item. But hold on, don't get upset. I wouldn't do that." The Answerer had held back from repeating the world dear, and she was glad of it.

"Good." Outside the window, she saw a bird gliding or hovering or doing something birds do. She didn't know what kind of bird it was. Most were pigeons or seagulls, but this one wasn't. She saw a condom wrapper on the floor. Just yesterday, he had unwrapped that. Lazy fucker hadn't put it in the trash. Passionate fucker was too involved with her body to care. See, there was the uncertainty. There were 13 ways of looking at a condom wrapper, but he wouldn't get that joke.

The voice continued: "But, on the other hand, sometimes there is more than one. Sometimes we think it's just one, but there are more along the way."

Is this part of the script or were they just talking—just words? They supposedly never engage in small talk. But they were right about this. There were many questions whirling in her head, and if she asked each one individually, it would cost a fortune. Was he right for her? Was she right for him? Should she date other people? Was it okay to have kind of boring sex if the person was really nice and you liked them in all the other ways?

But really, it boiled down to—should she be with him or not? Right? Just the one question and the voice on the phone. The person in a chair, most likely, a cup of tea beside them, the proprietary database at their fingertips. If they were even human. Who knew? They knew. The right answers.

Keep it simple, she told herself.

She hadn't used the Answering Service since college. Everyone did now. And people raved about how much easier it was. All of that doubt and confusion and second-guessing yourself were dumped from your mind.

On the side of the bed was a book that he had given her yesterday: *Preliminary Findings on the Order of Decisions*, a book that was propaganda from the other camp, the ones who thought we should be doing this all ourselves, who thought that the individual effort was what mattered. That there was something inherently good about doing it. She doubted that very much. What seemed to matter here was the outcome. A good decision. That's all anyone really ever wanted, and if someone else was better equipped to make it than she was, and it would save her all of that mental ping-pong, then why not.

On their second date, her boyfriend had told her that he never used the Answering Service. He told her he hated it. She found out later that his ex-girlfriend had used the service to decide to have an affair and then to decide to leave him for Brett, the other guy.

"They told her to do it," he said, his voice rising in anger tinged with pain that he never usually expressed. "Who would tell someone to do that? They told her to lie to me, and they pretend they are such good decision makers. Decision makers for the highest good. How can that possibly be true?"

"Mmmmmm," she patted his hand. "That's terrible."

But in her mind, she could construct a mental argument for the other side. Was his ex-girlfriend happier with this other man? And here he was with her, feeling, or saying, at least, that she was the BEST THING that had ever happened to him. So, if he really felt that, then maybe it was for the best, this immoral decision.

She also felt somewhat excited by the possibility that the Answering Service might tell her to do immoral or even illegal things. They weren't just following the rules, she thought, they were making judgments, and judgments were beyond the rules. It wasn't just an algo-rithm like some people thought. Just a com-puter thing. It really was unique in each case.

"So," the voice said, "are you ready to make a purchase?"

"Yes," she said, "I think so. How much infor-mation do you need?"

"Start with the item, and then I will ask for additional information as needed. Sometimes I need a little, and sometimes a lot."

"OK," she said, her voice quiet, guilty, as if he could hear although he was all the way across town. "Should I break up with my boyfriend? His name is Frank Sweran."

"Yes."

She thought there had been a mistake. "Yes ... what? Yes, you heard the question?"

"Yes," they said, "you should break up with your boyfriend."

She was surprised. What kind of service was this? It was so fast! When she asked about col-lege, they spent two hours going through all of the choices, where they were located, the cost, the majors, before the man (this was before they became gender-neutral) told her where to go. And here this person, this Answerer was just saying "Yes" after a few seconds. Not even enough time to shake a Magic Eight Ball.

"But how can you know if I don't tell you the story?" she asked.

Their voice was curt and pointed. "Each in-stance is different. Sometimes we need a lot of details, and sometimes we don't."

"But he's really nice to me."

"That's good to hear," they said, "and yet I don't need to know that."

"He is madly in love with me," she said. "He buys me books, and he picked me some random flowers on the way to my house. I think they were Queen Anne's Lace. They made my nose itch a little, but it was sweet." She felt, some-how, a kind of loyalty to him now. How could the Answerer dismiss Frank in just seconds? They had five months together. His saliva was mixed with hers, in her body even now, even if his semen had always been neatly tied up.

"We appreciate your business," the Answerer said, trying to give her the brush-off. "You will be billed for the product. It's been sold. It's up to you if you want to use the purchase."

"You mean, not follow the advice? How many people do that?" It wasn't something that she considered. Everyone said that the Answerers were the best, that it was silly to try to answer on your own when we had this option. It was really the money that kept her from using the service more, not because she doubted that the answers were the right ones.

"I have no way of knowing what percentage of people do not use the answers. Some items might go unused. Also, please be aware you have tried to purchase two more items in the last minute. Number one: 'How can you know if you haven't heard the story?' And number two,

'How many people do that?' As I said, I am not unscrupulous about such matters, but if you attempt to buy another item, I will have to sell it to you. For now I need to manually take those items out of your basket."

"Hold on! I'm just asking about my purchase already made. To see if it's worth it." She was getting a little pissed off.

"Would you like to be connected with customer service?" Their voice was just an octave off from calm. Were they even human? There were rumors that they had merged with the database long ago, but she had dismissed this as fake news.

"No, don't charge me, please. Just give me an idea how you decide."

"Have you read the procedures we use? Because before calling, we ask everyone on the website to agree that they have read all of the terms of agreement. On the website, under contractual obligations, see the language about factors in your life, verbal cues, larger societal statistics, biographical information, a complete database search of relevant information, current understandings of happiness and common-sense best judgment, demographic predictors of happiness, the Rule of Limited Options, the Platypus Proposition, Sidney's Secret Sauce (named after our founder Sydney Lott), and grandmothers' collective best advice. Those are the basic outlines of how we create our products. Others are trade secrets and cannot be divulged, but I assure you they are based on the most up-to-date research. Is that all for today?" they asked in a voice straining to be bright and chirpy, like a cartoon bird with its head sticking out of the cat's mouth.

"I guess so." She hung up.

She could still smell his scent in the bed sheets. She liked the way he smelled like a raisin mixed with iced tea. He had laughed when she told him that.

"Who could ever smell like that?"

"Only you, I guess," she laughed, and she remembered being truly happy in that moment. For at least that moment.

He had put his hand on her hair and petted it, then he stopped at her cheek and caressed it. She felt like a little girl.

And here it was before her: a $5oo purchase. It was supposed to make it easy. Of course, she should listen to them. This was what the Answerer was trained for. Perhaps they had more information than she gave them credit for. Maybe they had found something on Frank in the database, something that made him unequivocally a bad boyfriend. They might have had time to search his name.

She opened the book he had given her. A passage jumped out at her: "In human history, the ability to make decisions for yourself has been an important part of the evolution of the human race. A decision is a choice that leads us towards happiness or sorrow, life or death. People historically have fought to hold onto the ability to make decisions for themselves."

Fucking propaganda! She slammed the book shut. Where had all of those decisions in human history gotten us? Economic, environmental, and moral decay. People simply were not made to make decisions based on the limited information of one person, one history, one set of ideas. Or on something as nebulous and fleeting as human emotions—a cocktail of endorphins, adrenaline, dopamine, serotonin, and oxytocin. It was preposterous that humans had ever considered that a good idea.

The item in the basket has been purchased. She tossed the book on the floor, and would gather up his other things later and add them to the pile. She could pay an extra $5o dollars for the service to give him a call with the message, but she didn't want to be too impersonal. She would text him herself.

She was thirsty. She had sparkling water and iced tea in the refrigerator. She decided on the sparkling water.

♥

You Can Take It From Here

By Marguerite Hogan

ANGEL HADN'T seen a condom in years. But the sight of them, colorful and glossy in a clear glass bowl on the counter of the unisex bathroom, made her feel oddly nostalgic. They held her the way sunlight grazing the glass surface of a full gumball machine had held her as a child. Her mouth began to water.

There were so many. Would they ever run out? I want one. Her hand twitched.

Without another thought, she plunged her fist straight into the bowl with such enthusiasm that her knuckles struck the bottom and forced several condoms out onto the counter. She wiggled her fingers until she settled on one. The round, rubber ring of the condom slid around inside its plastic wrapper as she closed her hand around it. Giddy, she tucked the condom into the cavernous pocket of her raincoat and fled.

As she returned to the apartment she shared with Chet, practical questions emerged. Where would she store the condom? What would she do with it? How would she explain it to Chet? They hadn't used condoms in years. So why did she have it?

For the next week, Angel obsessed about the condom's whereabouts, especially relative to Chet's whereabouts. She moved it around several times a day. She tried a shoebox on the top rack of the closet and the back of a drawer full of nails and appliance manuals.

Whenever she imagined Chet finding it, harsh words and spit flying, she imagined herself flustered, face burning, unable to explain. Panicked, she would scramble to find a better hiding place. And as she overturned pillows and reconfigured the contents of the kitchen cupboards, she began to wonder why she was so afraid? It was just an impulse, she told herself. Nothing more.

After a week of hiding the condom around the apartment, she decided it had to go.

"Keep me," Angel heard as she approached the trash can of a nearby park. Her eyes scrambled about for a face to match the voice, but the park was empty. Her heart began to pound so intensely the contents of her ribcage rattled.

She looked down at the condom. "Keep me," she heard it say.

"You're talking," she whispered.

"Keep me," the condom repeated. "You want to."

"My name is Geoffrey," he told her when they were alone in her car.

"Are you really talking or am I imagining this?" Angel glanced around the dark carport to make sure no one else was there.

"I'm really talking," the condom explained.

The voice was deep and resonant as it expanded into the stale air of the car. She imagined an Adam's apple rolling beneath the velvety skin of a man's neck when he swallowed. She imagined him looking into her eyes intently. And she suppressed a shiver.

"How is that possible?"

"Everything is possible," he winked. "You know that."

"Not this," she laughed and shook her head.

"Have it your way," he shrugged.

"Tell me something you've never told anyone," Geoffrey said.

They were in Angel's parked car again and she was resting her bare feet on the steering wheel while Geoffrey balanced on her left knee cap.

She thought for awhile. "I can't think of

anything.”

“Tell me about your first date then.”

“It was with Chet. In high school.”

“And?” he prodded.

“That’s it,” she said, trying to recall the name of the movie.

“That’s it?” Geoffrey cocked his head to one side and raised an eyebrow.

“I’m sorry if that wasn’t interesting enough for you.” She tossed her hair and imagined him watching her.

“Was it interesting enough for you?”

She felt her stomach lurch and a stinging feeling of an unpleasant memory began to swell within her. Geoffrey sat patiently as if he already knew what she would say.

“About a year earlier,” she began slowly, “a boy asked for my phone number.”

“Can you blame him?” Geoffrey touched her cheek.

And her eyes filled with tears.

“Tell me why you’re crying,”

She imagined Geoffrey reclining, ankles crossed, gazing at her sweetly.

“I was really excited to tell my mother that a guy asked for my number,” she began. “I expected her to be proud. She always wanted to know who I liked and encouraged me to look as attractive as possible around him. She recommended fad diets. I thought the whole point was to get a guy’s attention. When I told her, she was washing dishes at the sink and had her back to me. But when she turned around, her face looked so hard, like it was about to crack. She asked a few questions about him and I told her what I knew, which wasn't much. Because I wasn't really interested in him. I was just doing what I thought she wanted me to do."

Angel could feel the grainy skin of Geoffrey's fingertips stroking her wrist.

"And then what happened?" he asked.

"Then," her voice cracked. "She called me a slut. Because I gave a boy my phone number." Tears cascaded over her jaw, down her neck and into the crevices of her collarbone. She dropped her chin to her chest.

"It's okay," Geoffrey said. And she imagined his arms snug around her, the warm air circulating between her open mouth and his bare neck, her runny nose darkening his collar with streaks of snot.

Angel sniffled. "There's more."

"I'm still listening," Geoffrey whispered.

"I was so stunned and embarrassed that I turned to walk away from her. But before I could take a step, something smacked me in the back of my head. I heard a loud bang as it hit the floor."

She pressed her face firmly into the skin of Geoffrey's neck as the bristles of his stubble imprinted on her balmy forehead. He cupped the back of her head with his large palm. She could hear the crunch of her hair giving way to his fingers.

"It was a bottle of dish soap," Angel sobbed. "And then she called me a slut again."

"There's no such thing as a slut," Geoffrey said.

"I know that now," Angel wiped her tears with the back of her hand. Then she added, "But I married the first guy I dated just to show her that I wasn't."

They sat in silence for awhile.

"I've never told anyone that before," Angel confessed.

"Not even Chet?"

"Not even Chet."

"Who named you Geoffrey?" Angel mused as she traced the letters on the surface of Geoffrey's wrapper while he reclined against the mound of her thumb. She imagined him moaning softly on his exhale. They were parked in their usual spot.

"I did," Geoffrey said. "Who named you Angel?" She heard the rustle of his jeans against the taut fabric of the passenger seat as he turned toward her and leaned closer.

"My mother."

"What would you have named yourself?"

Angel nearly snorted. "What a silly question! Why does it matter?"

"Why does it matter what someone else named you?"

She shrugged. "You have a point. But I like my name. Who doesn't like angels?"

"I love angels." Geoffrey's voice vibrated

softly. She felt the jagged callouses of his palm scuff her knuckles as he covered her hand with his and slowly interlaced their fingers. The heat of his touch crawled up her arm like a vine.

"If only I was one," her voice broke suddenly.

"Aren't you?" Geoffrey probed. She could feel the humidity of his breath as he looked down at her, lips slightly parted to reveal the bumpy, white bottoms of his two front teeth. She imagined his tongue, hovering just behind them, coarse and damp.

"I've gotten so many conflicting messages," Angel sighed as Geoffrey hummed lightly, stroking her ear, then her jaw, fingertips grazing her neck. "It's all so confusing," she sniffled.

"What part?"

"All of it. I'm an angel. I'm a slut. I'm talking to a condom."

"Yes, no, maybe so. But nobody else can tell you what you are."

"Are you cheating on me?" Chet demanded, banging his open palms against the table.

"No," Angel said firmly.

"Then who the hell is Geoffrey?"

"I already told you. This is Geoffrey," she motioned toward the condom lying on the table between them.

Chet snorted in annoyance. "And why did you name him that?"

"He named himself."

"Please be serious." Chet's voice was stern,

the wrinkles around his eyes looked more entrenched than usual.

"I know it sounds crazy. But I promise I'm not cheating on you."

"Why are you carrying around a condom, then?"

She held her breath.

"Were you thinking about cheating on me?"

"Probably not?"

Chet rolled his eyes. "And then the condom started talking to you?"

Angel nodded enthusiastically.

"Ridiculous," he groaned wearily. And then a moment later: "But I believe you."

"You do?" She squeaked and sat upright, feeling a surge of gratitude.

"I believe that you're not cheating on me," he pushed his chair back from the table. "But I don't believe the condom is talking to you. You need help."

Chet rose and started to turn away.

"Where are you going?" Angel resisted the urge to grab for his arm.

"I don't have anything more to say." His back was to her now.

"But I do," she said as assertively as she could.

"Does Chet know about me?" Geoffrey had asked one afternoon.

"Of course not," Angel had snapped back at him. "How would I explain this?"

"Just tell him the truth."

"I don't even know what that is."

"I think you do," he nudged her shoulder gently.

She leaned closer to him and inhaled the distinct scent of his aftershave. "Geoffrey," she said a few minutes later. "I love you."

Geoffrey didn't answer.

"Go on." Chet's voice was sharp. He was standing beside the table now, arms crossed over his broad chest.

"I just need a minute."

She scooped up Geoffrey in both palms and turned away from Chet.

"Geoffrey," she raised her hands to her face and whispered to the condom. "Please. Just talk to me one more time. I can't do this without you."

She stared down at the crinkled plastic, scuffed now.

"You can take it from here," she thought she heard it say. "Did you hear that?" She turned to Chet abruptly.

"You begged a condom to talk to you." Chet frowned. "Please get on with this."

She looked back at Geoffrey. "You can take it from here," she heard again. But it wasn't Geoffrey's voice this time. It was her own. She dropped the condom and turned back to Chet.

"I want a divorce," she announced.

Your Invisible Neighbor
By Claire Anderson

YOUR INVISIBLE neighbor rarely leaves his house. So you assume.

When he does leave his house, your invisible neighbor is usually wearing only a few articles of clothing at a time. A hat, some gloves in the winter, shoes (of course!), and maybe a jaunty little scarf or ascot, those year-round because they're fashionable. Only with gloves on can you tell if he's waving back at you.

When he walks his dog—his visible dog—all you can really see of him passing you by on the street is a floating leash attached to his dog's collar. It's funny when the dog suddenly pulls left or right, because the floating leash just whips and zooms away with him, and you have to imagine the expression on your invisible neighbor's face.

Your invisible neighbor's dog is named Herbert George, after the H.G. in H.G. Wells, who once wrote a book he called The Invisible Man. Your invisible neighbor loves that book. You gave him a really nice copy of it a few Christmases ago, one all decorated with silver on the front. You're pretty sure he really appreciated it, but since you couldn't see his face you're not totally sure. But he sounded pleased.

Your invisible neighbor doesn't talk much. Or at least, not to you. He seems to prefer the solitude of being, you guess, the only invisible man in a very visible neighborhood. You wonder sometimes if he doesn't get lonely, all invisible and alone with his dog and his house, but when you do talk to each other, he seems nothing but cheerful.

You find your invisible neighbor kind of funny, even if—and I agree with you here—he is a little weird. But maybe he has the right to be weird. Maybe it's right for him. There seems to be no one in the whole world the exact same kind of weird as him. And that's sort of beautiful.

When you need your invisible neighbor's help with something, or have a favor to ask him, he's always got your back. He must be—at least a little bit—super strong, because he is a master at moving furniture around. He's rearranged your living room five times already, single-handedly! Your invisible neighbor says he's always happy to help. He says that's what neighbors are for.

You've never asked him how he became invisible, or if he's always been invisible, and you probably never will. It doesn't feel appropriate. You don't want your precious few conversations to get too uncomfortable. But still, your mind likes to wander. Was it some kind of nuclear testing accident? A voluntary experiment gone wrong? Was he born invisible? Are either of his parents invisible?

He's never mentioned his family before, and he never has visitors or travels anywhere for the holidays. You wonder.

You think about your invisible neighbor often, and sometimes with unexpected fondness. You hope he thinks about you, too, but you doubt he does. You're used to doubting.

When the doorbell rings one day when it's raining and you open the front door to see a trench coat, boots and gloves attempting to close a wet umbrella while wrangling a dog and his floating leash, after you pull them both inside and your invisible neighbor tells you all about how he's locked himself out of the house, how silly of him, but could he and Herbert George please dry off and warm up in your lovely home because you're the neighbor they know best, and could your invisible neighbor use your phone to call a locksmith, and once he's done that he tells you how the locksmith is charging extra for having to drive so far uptown and in this rain of all things; when all this happens, you finally realize you're in love with your invisible neighbor.

And when, a little while later, you're sitting together talking by the fireplace, snoring dog calm on the rug between your armchairs, sipping hot tea that you can just see going into the place where your invisible neighbor's mouth should be, in the middle of a casual conversation that somehow went from stories about losing keys to an analysis of Oscar Wilde and 19th century morals, after you accidentally mention something you've noticed about how your invisible neighbor likes to keep his rose garden, something he says no one's ever noticed before; at that moment, without really saying it yet, your invisible neighbor tells you he loves you, too.

Technicolor
By Enya Mayne

WHEN I see his face, I know I'm in trouble.

Incandescent smile, with almost too many teeth. Wide-set eyes downturned at the corners, glossy-bright. Scrappy build, muscles ropy from hoisting around 25-kilo bags of soil.

He blinks, like my face is a light his eyes need to adjust to. He smells like coconut sunscreen and mulch. And he is stubbornly staying black-and-white.

"Your eyes..." He squints. "They're even more beautiful in color."

"Thank you," I say, and tuck a frizzled lock of hair behind my ear. Momma told me my eyes were the color of sea glass, just like Dad's. To me, they were the same pale gray as dishwater.

"My name's Roan," the boy says, and holds out a hand. His palm is thick with calluses, his nails crusted with dirt. I rub my eyes, and look to see if color is blooming in his irises.

But his eyes remain slate gray. A spatter of freckles highlights the apples of his cheeks, where the sun kissed him.

"I'm Gemma." I point down at my name tag. "It's my first day."

"Gemma." He searches my face. "I should tell you, the second I saw you, I saw the green of your eyes. Did it happen for you?"

Momma had promised me my Technicolor moment would come. The moment I'd meet the One, and my world would explode with flashes of color like overexposed film.

Boys who made my heart skitter. Girls who sent a flush creeping up my face. None of them had exploded with color. Not yet.

I dig my nails into my wrist, willing myself to see the color of Roan's checkered shirt, the hue of his eyes. Surely, concentration would saturate my world with every shade of the rainbow.

"It's not happening," I say, and his face ashes over. "I'm sorry."

"Don't worry." He has one pronounced dimple; his smile is crooked. There's a piece of gray grass tangled in his nest of hair, but I don't tell him. "Have you ever worked at a plant nursery before? I can show you the ropes."

The whole day he guides me around, explains how to water the ferns, tells me which bushes are particularly temperamental. But he spends half his time gaping at the flowers.

"I wish you could see." He grazes the petal of a petunia with a careful finger. "I always heard about the Technicolor moment. But no one told me this could happen. That it could be unrequited."

Roan drives me home in his rusty silver pickup truck, asks me rapid-fire questions. Tells me about his parents, who had their Technicolor moment at a house party.

"My mom's first comment to my dad was that his shoes didn't match his belt." Roan chuckles. "But then, they fell out of love, and they Faded. Back to black and white. Maybe that's even sadder than my unrequited Technicolor moment."

When I get home, Momma's waiting at the kitchen table, painting her long nails. Momma's skin is onyx, her cheekbones just as sharp. Dad's is alabaster-pale. Mine lies somewhere in the middle. A rare gem, Momma always said.

"How was your first day?" she asks, her tongue poking out like it did when she was focused. I wonder what color her polish is today. They're all still a spectrum of gray in my eyes.

"I met a boy," I say. She glances up from her manicure, eyebrows quirked. I shake my head. "He had his moment, when he saw me. I really like him. But it's all still gray to me."

"Oh, sweetie. Be patient," she says, and pats

the chair beside her. "Don't rush into things. Not unless the person makes the sunset glow in orange and violet. Not until they flood your vision with color. These things take time. You deserve the best, my precious gem."

Easy for her to say. She'd seen Dad's eyes, glowing phosphorescent green across her high school cafeteria and known he was the One. What if my world stays black and white forever? What if my heart is tar-black, incapable of love?

The next day, rain drizzles down from fat clouds, mist goosebumps my arms. It's the kind of day that would be gray, even for the lucky Technicolor lovers.

Roan smiles at me when I arrive at the nursery. Even if he's still monochrome, he makes my stomach swoop acrobatic. As we work, repotting and chatting and digging and laughing, I forget to worry about color.

He drives me home again that night, the rain falling in sheets and flooding the bed of his truck. His hands patter against the steering wheel. He's the kind of guy who talks with wild hand gestures; his movements are a richer language than his words.

"So." He glances at me, a hopeful gleam in his eyes. "No Technicolor yet?"

He doesn't notice the curve in the road, and by the time he does, the rain makes it too slick for him to adjust. Tinnitus fills my head; the smell of burnt rubber and dust stings my nostrils.

Roan's hair glimmers with broken glass, a sparkling crown. He moans. His neck pulses slippery with blood.

"You're okay," I say, but my voice wilts. My airbag pins me against my seat, and I unclip my seatbelt to help him.

I press my hands to his jugular, stem the flow of blood. The deep red sears my eyes. It's blinding, too beautiful.

"Roan," I whisper. "It happened."

His lips are the dusky rose color of the sunsets Momma always described. He smiles.

♥

Protection Spell
By Loren Rhoads

STELLA WAKES in the night, but Alondra is asleep. Alondra can sleep through anything these days. After too many years of insomnia, she has finally learned to rest.

Stella's not sure what woke her. Was there a noise? Despite the summer heat, the hotel room has turned very cold. She is surprised to see her breath plume out in front of her.

And part around a face looming above her. But the face isn't there. No one is there. The room is empty, save for Alondra, asleep, and Stella, absolutely frozen in place.

An invisible weight sinks onto the mattress beside Stella's legs. The weight presses against her thigh, only the sheet and a thin wool blanket to shield her.

The invisible body burns colder. Stella shivers, but she cannot move. She cannot push the unwanted intrusion away. She tries to remember what to do, what to say, what to think. Alondra would know. If she were awake, Alondra would protect Stella.

An idea that isn't hers twines amidst Stella's thoughts:

If she loved you, she'd wake up. She would keep you safe, if she loved you.

Stella hears herself make a sound. It's meant to be a protest, but it sounds as if it's coming from a frightened child. Stella hates the violation of this haunting: in her space, in her thoughts, in their bed. And Stella realizes that she can't feel Alondra beside her any longer. It's as if she is alone in this unfamiliar bed in this unfamiliar room in an unfamiliar hotel. She knew it had been a brothel back in the Gold Rush days. Did someone die here? Is that someone trapped here now?

As if to comfort her, Alondra's body shifts, snuggles against Stella, slides her arm around Stella's waist.

"Cold," Alondra murmurs sleepily.

"Ghost," Stella answers softly.

"Oh." Alondra's lips brush Stella's neck. Stella isn't sure if Alondra is awake when she suggests, "Kiss me?"

Stella turns her face down toward Alondra's. What a relief to be able to move again. She closes her eyes against the plumes of breath, the invisible face, the icy weight, the aching, lonely, jealous dead.

Stella breathes deeply, inhaling the faintest scent of Alondra's perfume — orange and clove, protection and fire — and she kisses this wonderful, magical woman who came into her life and made everything real: fairies and ghosts, sylphs and mermaids, spirits and spells and love.

Stella leans into the kiss and feels its power, like slipping into a hot bath, shimmer across her skin in a web of light.

They haven't come here to hunt ghosts, Stella thinks. This is meant to be a vacation for Alondra, a respite from the constant requests for help, the demands of people and supernatural beings drawn to Alondra's light.

Stella sighs with frustration. She doesn't want to burden Alondra, doesn't want to need her help, but her flesh warms at Alondra's touch. She feels the glow of Alondra's perfume—however faint—settle around her like sunshine.

The ghost shifts beside Stella, moving away as if rising to stand beside the bed. Stella catches a glimpse: It is a woman, her hair twisted into a disheveled pile atop her head, the satin of her corset frayed and stained.

The ghost bends toward them—not looming: yearning. Stella wonders who the ghost had loved. Had they been able to be honest with each other? Had they been able to tell the world? Did she haunt this room because this was where they had been safe together? Aching pity fills Stella's heart. Now she feels a kinship with the ghost, but doesn't know how to help.

Alondra shifts again, fully awake. She holds out her hand. Pale wisps of fingers weave between hers.

"Go find her," Alondra says gently. "She's waiting for you."

The ghost, warmed by love, melts away.

"Why didn't you wake me?" Alondra asks.

Stella shakes her head and snuggles into Alondra's embrace. "You shouldn't have to work all the time."

"Love isn't work."

Stella can't think of a better answer than to kiss her again.

♥

Whose Woods Are These?

By Veronica Montes

SHE CASTS her small hands this way and that as she speaks: to her left towards the fog-shrouded mountains, then to the sky, the earth, the sea.

She stands barefoot on pine needles, erect and slim, conducting an orchestra that doesn't exist. Her hair falls past her narrow shoulders in loose, gray waves. Strands lift in the strong breeze. She is a lightning storm, a live wire.

"Why are you in my woods?" she screams. "What do you seek in my woods? Who sent you to my woods? What do you know of my woods?"

On and on, roaring and snarling and pointing at me: Why, what, who, who, who.

These are questions, but she presents them

as an incantation—a strange, insistent poem. She is old enough to be my grandmother, so I'm hesitant to hush her, but when she starts poking me in the shoulder I take a stand.

"Wait a minute, wait a minute, don't do that," I say. I grasp her hands to still them. Her manicure, I note, is impeccable; her nails are shell pink. "Who says these are your woods? Who told you that?"

"That man told me so," she says. She looks all around us at the pine, the cedar, the fir. Her eyes go soft. "He gave them to me as a gift." She grows shy, and I watch as the drooping curves of her face sharpen for a moment into what must have been a glorious youth. "He said, 'Only these woods can rival your beauty.'"

For a few moments she's lost in a reverie, and I look away because it's private, just hers. I stare instead at the top of my hiking boots, I crunch the forest detritus beneath them, I listen for birdsong.

Soon enough her hands reach for mine.

"Now, come here. Come closer," she urges. "I'll show you."

She reaches inside her shirt, somewhere near her heart, and produces a small photograph. The date stamp reads November 1971.

"Oh," I say. "Oh. I see."

I do the math quickly: the picture was taken fifty-two years ago. He's wearing striped bell bottoms and a ribbed turtleneck and suede zip-up boots. When I turn it over I recognize the familiar loops of his florid penmanship. *Love is forever*, it says. I toss the photo back to her like a hot potato, but it catches on the breeze and disappears. She doesn't seem to mind.

I'm not going to be mysterious about it: if you strip away the sideburns and Brady Bunch wardrobe, the man in her photo and the man I've been married to for eighteen years are the very same. It's best if you simply accept what I'm saying as fact and move on. If I can do it, you can, too.

We met ... well, what does it matter? What's important here is that when we pulled up to the edge of these goddamn woods he kissed me. He said he couldn't wait to finish up with his clients and meet me at the house he'd rented for the weekend. He gave me a hand-drawn map with a trail of hearts leading to the cabin. And on the back?

Love is forever.

When I was young ... well, what does it matter? I had the sensibility of a peacock, is what I want to say. The red lipstick, the glittered décolletage, my shining hair, my big, clear eyes. I'm not an unreasonable person: I understand the fleeting nature of beauty, and when mine sputtered to its end I was happy to have had my fill. As the years passed I became more owl than peacock, my dulled feathers camouflaged by tree bark, my head cocked at strange angles, invisible.

All the while he stayed the same. I grew to

love the dark. I thought he didn't mind.

I turned to leave, and the woman threw a rock at me. She was shockingly strong and accurate.

"Hey!" I said to the woman. "What was that for?"

She shrugged. "The woods aren't big enough for both of us."

"You're awful. Do you hear me? You awful, awful, hag."

She laughed, then. Not the cackling sound you'd expect in a story like this, but a full-throated, resonant laugh. It made me feel suddenly tender towards her.

"I'm sorry," I said. "I didn't mean that."

My apology awakened a different version of her. She snapped out of her semi-stupor and twisted her hair into a knot at the top of her head. She cocked a hip and crossed her arms.

"Another one came before you, you know."

"I figured."

"And there'll be another one after you." She flinches at this, as if it hurts her more than it hurts me. Maybe it does.

"Right. I'm clear on that."

"Take the rock," she said. "Safeguard our woods."

I checked to make sure I'd heard her correctly. "Whose woods?" I said.

"Oh so now you're a smart ass. I said 'ours.' Our woods."

"Got it. Yes. I'll safeguard our woods." I bent

down to retrieve the rock, and then I picked up another and another and another until my backpack was full, but not too heavy to carry. "Anything else?" I asked.

"He won't be back for another ten, maybe fifteen, years. I probably won't be here," she said. "So you should find the others. They can help you."

"I'll be okay," I tell her. "Don't worry."

"Aim for his head," she said.

Rendezvous at the Pier
By Joe Belarge

TREVOR HAD never dated a real woman, which is how he knew Marie was a bot.

A real woman would never build an avatar with pimples, knobby knees, and cellulite. A real woman wouldn't walk hand-in-hand with Trevor for hours, gliding through crowds of glittering avatars in virtual LA, showered in the luster of perpetual digital sunshine, and leave the function enabled that allowed sweat from her palm to slick the inside of his haptic glove.

No, Marie was just too unbelievable, and that was a real shame, because Trevor had enjoyed the last six months quite a bit.

Leading Marie off the digital boardwalk, Trevor sat across from her on the lush grass.

Neon palm fronds swayed in the breeze and dappled their avatars with dancing shadows. Trevor's haptic fan shook beneath him and warm air glided over his arms, into his hair. Bursts of lavender aerosoled from Trevor's haptic chair, and the faint, perfectly irregular crash of ocean waves sounded in his HUD-helmet.

"I think we should see other people."

"What d'you mean?" Marie asked.

"The thing is," Trevor said, leaning in. His virtual biceps bulged in the lower half of his HUD. He flexed and wondered not for the first time which company had programmed Marie to repeatedly say she didn't like his muscles.

"God, are you checking yourself out?" Marie spat. "You know what, fine—"

"Wait," Trevor said. "It's nothing personal, it's just that … I know."

That's what he said every time. Even though they weren't humans it somehow seemed impolite to call them bots to their faces. Marie's brows knit and her eyes rendered blood red. Shiny tears slid down her blemished cheeks.

"Don't know what I expected," she grumbled. Walking away, she called over her shoulder: "You're all the same."

The comment twisted in Trevor's gut. Having his data mined was one thing, but he expected the bots he dated to accept him breaking the relationship with some grace.

"I'd like to submit a one-star review, your bot is—"

"What?" Marie spun, tears gone, veins bulging in her neck and her face now rendered crimson. "You think I'm a bot?"

The pain in Trevor's stomach tightened into a familiar knot, the one that plagued him at night after he'd shed his haptic suit and lay alone, wondering how many of his ideas were his own, and how many were subliminally fed to him; wondering if any of his relationships were real, or if they ever would be.

"Nothing? Typical. If you've got any balls, meet me at the Santa Monica Pier in two hours. I'll be on the broken Ferris wheel. You'll recognize me, cause I look like this," Marie jabbed a finger toward her face, then stalked away.

Trevor inhaled a burst of lavender aerosol from his haptic chair and waited for the knot in his stomach to loosen.

It didn't.

"All that, for what," he mumbled, powering down his haptic suit. "Data on my fetishes? What kind of food I fantasize about? These damn companies'll do anything for a buck."

Trevor removed the HUD-helmet and grimaced at the stale air pushing in on him. He stood and stretched. His joints creaked and his knuckles brushed the water-stained ceiling. Behind the haptic chair, gray sheets lay tangled on the bed. Stepping to his right, he opened the sustainment cabinet door and frowned at the three canisters of protein rations. He grabbed one, mixed in water from the steel sink, and sat crossways on his haptic chair. He tilted lumps of bland wet mush into his mouth, hoping eating would soothe his pain.

It didn't.

He tossed the canister in the sink. Sighing, Trevor straightened in his chair and wriggled into the haptic suit. A clock flashed as he signed on. An hour had passed since Marie left him. He laughed nervously to himself.

"She's full of shit," he muttered. "Just programmed to say that stuff so I'll go back to her, so they can collect more data, feed me more targeted ads."

Trevor ground his teeth. He needed to unwind the knot in his gut. He needed to see Marie. He needed to apologize. He'd never apologized to a bot before.

Trevor accessed the map and searched for Marie. A box flashed saying he'd been blocked.

The knot tightened.

What if Marie was real?

What if he met her, felt the true warmth of her hand in his?

The world spun. Trevor reached out to steady himself and grabbed air. The knot in his stomach seized once, then again, convulsing until bitter mush leapt in his throat and he puked into his HUD-helmet.

"Shit," Trevor said. He powered down and peeled off the suit and shuffled to the sink to clean up. He pulled off his shirt, saw the pale flab of his arms, the narrow hunch of his shoulders. Sores dotted his torso from his haptic suit.

Trevor splashed cool water on his face, then opened a small drawer under his bed and grabbed a clean shirt. He turned back to his haptic chair. A sour stench rose from the suit and clung to the walls. Bile surged again in his throat and he rushed out onto the apartment landing.

Doubled over, he gulped crisp air.

"Goddammit, she's not real," he gasped. "I'm real. *I am real.*"

♥

Phase

By Jyotsna Sreenivasan

HIS WIFE is asleep when he slips out of bed, drawn by an urge he can't name. The new baby nestles by her side. He leans over the child and sniffs its neck. Milky. Yet too small. Downstairs, he opens the back door and frowns. Why is he exiting his suburban house in the middle of the night in his pajamas and bare feet?

But once he steps into the watch of the cold circle of the moon, he does not find it odd that claws sprout from his toes. He runs his tongue over his teeth, satisfied with the new long canines. His feet tread over the manicured lawn, through the tangle of brush at the back of the lot, and down to the ravine. He lopes easily over crackling leaves and twigs. The icy spring night cannot bite through his fur. His lungs suck in streams of frosty air. When his nose finds what it wants, he stops at a dense thicket. Sensing the first hot shaft of fear from the doe, he pounces on the soft spotted fawn. The doe flees. He'll find her on another night.

Sated, leaving clean bones scattered, he retreats. The moon has arced across the black sky. As the first blush of dawn appears in the east, he steps inside and shuts the door. His pajamas hang in rags around him.

"Honey?" Her hair sleep-tousled, she appears at the top of the stairs. "Did you sleep-walk outside again?"

He climbs towards her. The baby in her arms looks tender.

"Are you bleeding?" she asks.

He holds up his hands, streaked with rust. "I'm OK. Just dirty." He strips off his clothes in the upstairs hallway.

She wrinkles her nose. "You smell like ... like ..." She presses the baby's head to her chest. "This is the second time. You said it wasn't going to happen again."

"I need a shower. And a nap."

She squints at him as he disappears into the bathroom. "I'll go make breakfast," she whispers to the closed door.

After starting the coffee maker she creeps back upstairs, still clutching the child, and gazes at him asleep. Cautiously, she touches his cheek, strokes his hair. He snorts softly.

In the hallway, she swipes up the scraps of muddy, reeking clothing and runs downstairs, the infant snuggled in the crook of her arm. He'll be fine. He's just going through a phase. The first time was a month ago, soon after the child's birth. It must be the stress of being a new parent. Things will settle down soon. She stuffs the rags into the trash can in the garage. He said he was OK. She needs to believe him.

She peers out the open garage door into the morning air. The baby waves its tiny hand towards the sunshine.

♥

Supernova

By Brittani Jenee' Cal

THE FIRST time I met Natalia, she smelled so much like uranium I thought the star inside my chest would explode.

She wore a blue dress, and sunlight clung to her in a way that made me wonder if my hands would leave burn marks on her skin. She looked up at me with those two orbiting moons, and the entire universe shifted.

"I was wondering when you would find me," she said.

It was the first time I heard her laugh. She laughed so much in those days, before she started to forget this was all a dream.

When the memory loss started, I took her to the coast where the stars hid beneath the sea.

We drove through daylight, emerging beneath a sliver of moon in a black sky until the air was thick with salt. She ran ahead, leaving a trail of clothes for me to follow in the sand.

The water was warm, and the night was dark. We didn't see them at first. Not until I swam up beside her. Then each stroke, each kick, surrounded us in light. They luminated toward the surface in flashes of color, bursting from blackness as we swam through an unexplored galaxy. If we stopped moving, the water went dark, so I moved my arms and legs as much as I could, believing if there was enough light she would have to remember.

"Look," I said. "They know who we are."

"Phytoplankton," she said, and something inside me sank to the bottom of the ocean. "Bioluminescence, chemiluminescence ..."

She was speaking a language I couldn't understand, and with each word our bodies drifted further apart.

Years later, when the Perseids came, I drove us up into the mountains where the fluorescent lights of the city vanished. We lay on warm blankets and watched the stars stretch themselves like the bow of a cello. They fell from the sky while we fell in love with each other over and over. She kissed me in patterns that mirrored the movement of planets and hope burned in me until I thought I would explode.

Carbon. Hydrogen. Oxygen.

"They're orchestrating the sky for us," I said.

"Meteors," she said, and my chest dropped as heavy as a rock. "Chondrites, achondrites ..."

She was forgetting more and more of who we were with every word, clinging so tightly to this world it wasn't a dream for her anymore.

I needed her to remember.

I reached into my chest, grasping the star inside of it. It emerged without resistance, a glowing silver orb in my palm.

Natalia leaned into me, and the star shone brighter. A spark of memory flashed over her. She stared at it with wide eyes, then up at me.

"Make a wish on it," she said. "Wish that you could forget, too."

Her words burned a black hole in me where the star had been.

That's when I knew. She had wished to forget.

The last moments I spent with her, the brightest star she could remember leaked morning in through the window.

"Stay here with me," she said as she traced freckled constellations on my chest.

Her skin radiated heat. It promised to give me everything I could ever want in exchange for my memories.

For the rest of the morning, I gave them to her, tangled up in phosphorus and bedsheets, until every atom of energy had been expended. She fell beside me, pushing her soft cheek against my neck. Her eyes dripped with sunlight, burning the places it touched me, leaving blisters across my skin.

I'd kept the star out of my chest for too long. A violent collapse was happening inside me. It would take her by force if I stayed, waking us both from beautiful insignificance.

I gasped for air as my vision narrowed. And then, there they were. Shimmering through a tunnel of blackness as the world went dark.

"They're here," I said.

She laid her hand on top of mine.

"We'll go together," she said. "Make a wish."

We were part of an old universe, memories of an awakened Cosmos—but even still, as I imagined this world without Natalia in it, an immense pressure built up inside me.

I ripped our bodies away from one another.

She called out, but the sound was lost in the high-pitch ringing of the star. I cradled it in my hands, holding it as far from her as I could. White heat burned through me.

I looked at her one last time, begging some part of me to remember her this way.

Then I closed my eyes
took a deep breath
and wished that I would wake up.

Helium. Nitrogen. Dust.

♥

EmoMo

By Liam Hogan

I SNAPPED on the hall light as Alfred bumbled through the front door. He turned and blinked owlishly, coat buttoned out of step, scarf a snake frantic to strangle him.

"You'd better have a bloody good excuse for being late!"

Alfred blinked again. And then—and then!—he began to grin.

"Actually, dear, I rather suppose I *do*."

He was carrying something. Something he hadn't left the house with, all those hours ago. Something like ... a *pet* carrier? As if to make sure I'd gotten the point, Alfred waved the crate in the air, and then, as mewling started from within, made shushing, cooing noises.

I glowered. I'd spent an hour getting ready, and then another hour getting angry. Whereas Alfred appeared to have had time to drop in on a pet menagerie, and no time at all to brush his hair or even polish his glasses.

"What. Is. *That?*" I demanded, each punctuation a stab with a sharp knife.

"This," Alfred said, "is an EmoMo." He unlatched the crate and lifted a thin, mottled-grey creature, blinking myopically and all too familiarly into the light. He'd chosen a pet that looked as useless as he did.

"A what?"

"An Emotion-Morph. An alien with incredibly adaptable genetics. It changes shape and form in response to the emotions around it."

"Whose emotions?" I snapped. "Yours, or mine?"

"Well, *both*: that's the point," Alfred said. "It reveals any hidden tension in the air."

"Then it's not bloody—"

But I didn't get to say *working*, because Alfred let loose a yelp. The EmoMo dropped to the floor and scurried towards me, growing porcupine quills as it did.

When the relationship counsellor suggested we try "date nights," an evening once a week when we would try not to bite each other's heads off, I'd loathed the idea. It felt so forced, so fake, so ... *American*. But Alfred had agreed to the proposal, and I could hardly be the one to put the spanner in the works, could I?

I'd assumed—and dressed for—something like dinner at a nice little eatery, the sort of place we'd gone to when we first met. And, like those olden, fools-golden days, I'd left the choosing and booking to Alfred.

Somehow, and I really wasn't sure how, that had been translated into him bringing home a mutant beast, currently alternating between hissing and blinking as it padded back and forth between us.

"Explain," I demanded.

"I was talking to Johnson over lunch—"

I narrowed my eyes. Thin. Ice. Alfred seemed to belatedly realise the danger of discussing his marital strife with work colleagues, or at least of me finding out.

"Ah, and," he blustered, "Johnson and Greg have been going through their own sticky patch, if you will, and he swore by their EmoMo, and said I could borrow it. For date nights?"

Thereby ensuring our so-called date nights didn't involve leaving the house. We could hardly take such a prickly, unpredictable animal to a restaurant, or a theatre, or even the cinema. I shook my head.

"If it's so bloody *great*, why did he give it to *us*?"

Alfred blushed. "Um ... The reason an EmoMo mimics the emotions of others is so that it can get closer to them ..."

I looked down to where the EmoMo was nestled against my best going-out boots. It better not mark the leather.

"*And?*"

"And … then it feeds on their emotions."

"You're telling me you brought an alien *para-site* into our home?"

The porcupine spines were red tipped, almost as incandescent with rage as I felt.

"No, no, not a parasite … It feeds on strong emotions, but it doesn't suck them *out* of you. And Johnson and Greg … since they got their EmoMo, they've been so contented, that …"

"That *what?*"

"That the poor fellow was wasting away."

Moments earlier, if I had had anything at hand to throw, I would have thrown it. Hard. I peered down again. The EmoMo peered up. Then it looked across at Alfred, gave a small wag of a tail that hadn't been there a minute ago. Awkward, disheveled, *good-natured* Alfred. So desperate to please that he could never say no, even if what was asked of him was ruinous for us both.

The EmoMo rubbed against my shin, with spines that were no longer poison tipped, spines that were hardly sharper than a scratch with a ragged fingernail.

The wide-eyed little tyke licked its lips, looked adoringly up at me — and *burped.*

♥

A New Pair of Lips

By Meg Pokrass and Jeff Friedman

ONE MORNING, his wife came downstairs with new lips, big and bright.

Frankly, a little scary, he thought.

She smiled at him, and he smiled back cautiously, not knowing what her lips intended. Then before he could react, she kissed him on his lips. Her kisses tasted like something radioactive, something that would burn in the earth for centuries after their deaths, their history together written in glowing rock.

She already felt earthy, but he was made of illness, effluvium oozing from his body, his breath a fog of aerosols. She kissed him again, and he nearly fainted.

"What's wrong?" she asked.

"It's just that we're not what we once were. There's something about us that is not us."

She flashed her lips at him, almost angrily. "We're better," she said. "Think of it that way."

He tried to think of it that way, but in so many ways, he was much worse, less capable of keeping up with her born again sexiness. She wrapped him in her arms and picked him up.

"Light as a feather," she said. "I could carry you across the threshold."

He looked down at her joyful face and tried to remember her great old smile, but the new smile had swallowed it.

♥

Mine Again

By Katie Kent

"I'M SORRY, but we're over. I don't love you anymore."

Evie can't even look me in the eye as she delivers the final blow. It's not the first time I've heard her say those words, but that doesn't make them hurt any less.

The first few times, I begged her to stay. Asked if the past six months meant nothing to her. Reminded her of the good times we'd had together. But nothing I say ever makes any difference. This time, I just walk away, forcing myself not to look back. I don't need to see her face light up as she texts her new girlfriend.

Sitting on my bed later, hugging my pillow, Evie's words still echoing through my mind, I question how many more times I can do this. My heart has been broken again and again, and each time is harder than the last.

Yet I already know the answer. I'll keep doing this until my body gives up.

Concentrating on the moment just before we first met, time rushes past me like I'm in a wind tunnel. I arrive in my body six months ago, steady myself against the wall, dab the blood from my nose, and swallow a couple of pills to stave off the ache that's starting to pound at my head. It wasn't this bad at first, but the more times I've traveled back, the worse these symptoms have become. I know I'm not supposed to manipulate time like this, but what else can I do? I've tried living without her, and this is nothing compared to the pain of that.

I walk around the corner towards the café where I'd first met Evie, my heart quickening as I approach the door.

Her head is down, reading a book as she sips her coffee. I take in her long, dark hair, admire the way the sun frames her face, and smile to myself as she traces through the pages with her finger. Even though I've lost count of the number of times I've observed her like this, it's almost like I'm seeing her for the first time.

"Is this seat taken?" I ask, my body flooded with adrenaline.

She looks up, and gives me that smile that's floored me from the start. "No. Please, sit down. I've never seen it so busy in here."

"Thank you," I say, dumping my bag on the floor. "I'm Hannah."

She twirls her hair around her finger, something that always makes me melt. Later, I'll find out she does that when she's nervous. I'm hit by a flashback of stroking her hair in bed — although can I really call it a flashback when it hasn't even happened yet?

"Nice to meet you, Hannah. My name is Evie."

I can already feel the chemistry between us, and can hardly believe she's the same girl who will dump me without even looking me in the eye.

I have a sudden urge to kiss her, but it will be a couple of weeks before that happens, and I need to be patient. I've tried rushing things before, and it never turns out well. I slide into the seat opposite her, ready to start our relationship for the umpteenth time.

It won't last; it never lasts. I've tried so many times to change the outcome — varying what I say to her, where we go on dates, and anything else I can think of, but it seems to be impossible. I've given up trying. Now I'm just living the same six months over and over again, as if I was an actor practicing a scene. Soon enough, she'll dump me for another woman.

But for now, she's mine again.

A Mercy
By Alethea Eason

I WALK down Castro Street, the collar of my coat pulled up to protect my neck. I've wrapped my wings around me like an overcoat. No one I pass is the wiser.

My splattered glasses and the headlights of the cars turn the street into an impressionist painting. I'm not used to the city or the traffic, and I am careful as I walk. Partly from the rain blinding me—whenever I meet Nick, a storm accompanies him—but also because my spirit is ahead of my feet.

I'm a winged agent for the Controller, as Nick once was. I could evoke the warmth of his lips, but I won't this evening. I've been told this is my last chance, or the Controller will send the ones whose wings look like bruises.

The Controller is not the merciful God, and

Nick and I are no longer angels. Nick was our best agent—legendary, actually—until he refused to dirty his hands anymore.

I get to 24th Street and the rain unleashes into a torrent. I step under the awning of the building, breathe, and offer a short prayer.

Couldn't Joy or Ambush be sent instead of me? Neither of them has a history.

No.

The word echoes through my head like the edge of a migraine. The Controller will not be swayed. My jeans are soaked as I turn up 28th and walk to the charming house, circa 1920s, with the tiny gate that protects the yard from dogs. I enter and close it behind me.

"Hello, Beatrice," Nick says as I turn around. "So it is today?"

He looks the same. But I, an agent of the Controller, still age, and for the first time in all of our meetings, I look older than he does. Not by much, but enough to make me check my vanity, the small, fleeting hope that he still would want to touch me.

Stop. You're here to do a job. I follow him over the threshold. My robe of lapis blue unfurls along with my wings. Emeralds plucked from the mines of Heaven appear in my earlobes.

The light that surrounds me makes him wince ever so slightly.

"Always five o'clock, Nick. And always so cold and gray."

Every visit is a roll of the dice. He has seduced me with his words and long walks in the icy world outside. When I've been weak he's coaxed me to tuck in my wings, so that I can pretend I am real—in the Earthly sense.

I chose this work because I thought it noble and right, to guide events toward justice on Earth. What I've found is that truth and goodness are relative. Nick understands. He listens to me the way no angel or agent has ever done.

And he's begged me to release him. Not just like that evening in Italy, when there was more than a kiss. I blush. God knows I still want to, in every way except the way he needs most.

I am a mercy, or could be if I'd just do my job. If I hadn't wiped the poison from my lips in Kyoto. If I hadn't loosened the cord around his neck too soon in Paris.

Nick has said the Controller is kind enough to send me. He has also said the Controller is cruel. I join him in front of the fire he's kindled. He places his hand on my arm, guilty as I am for wanting it there.

I pull away after letting his palm burn my skin. "Don't you miss the sun?" I ask. "The moon?"

I know the answer. I have listened to the stories of his wounded soul.

"Would you care for tea, Beatrice?"

I shake my head. If I delay, the other agents might arrive. I might even have to watch what they do.

"Business, then." He sits at his desk by the bay window. Outside, the passers-by look around in awe—a blizzard in San Francisco, for the weather has come to that. I lower myself into the armchair across from him, an expanse of wood and scattered papers between us.

I consider accepting the cup of tea. I could pick up one of the poems and ask him to read it. Or to tell him how efficient Ambush is at this sort of thing.

But—I would be unable to save him. I reach into my robe and pull out the Walther PPK, a weapon for spies in another century.

I've gotten this far before—poisoned lipstick, the spider-silk cord—but never so soon. I won't flinch. "Time's up, Nick."

His eyes lock on mine. His lips compress, and then he smiles. "My favorite was the misericorde in Florence. How you held it to my heart in the little vicolo while I fumbled around with those ridiculous skirts."

I stick to business. "The Controller has been patient with my failed attempts—for old time's sake, for the times you saved Earth from going over the brink, but no more." A flash of red passes through me. Good, the anger I need. "The scales have been tipped because of your stupid sense of ethics."

But the gun grows heavy in my hand. I long to set it down, join Nick on the other side of the table in a straddle, and forget that when I leave the others will come—agents who have grudges and who will make the end an ugly thing.

It's his turn. He repeats his justification, one I have heard with each visit, either in a whisper in my ear with the stiletto pricking his skin, or when he's held me in bed the many times I didn't even try to kill him.

"I grew tired, Beatrice, of the hypocrisy. Do you really think the Controller cares for humanity? After all, if justice will always triumph, doesn't that make the position redundant?" Nick points to the window. "My memories create this perpetual winter. If it were possible for me to end this myself, I would have long ago. You have been my only hope."

My being beats with the red pulse, but now I know why my anger runs so deeply. I didn't pull the cork that unleashed plagues. Or murdered junta leaders with my bare hands, so a nation might have a few years of peace before the next dictator.

Other than this one job, I've been assigned easier targets.

"The scales have tipped. Erasing you will eliminate some of the messier threads that unraveled."

"Beatrice." My name in his mouth feels like he's holding my soul. "Why is that weapon really in your hand?"

We hold each other's eyes. He once said my presence was his only solace.

"You are a mercy," he says at last.

My hand trembles. I want to close my eyes, but he deserves more than that.

I hesitate for the last time. His body jerks. A red flower blossoms on his white shirt.

Only I could give him this gift so kindly, I tell myself, wanting it to be true. It must be true because, as he fades away forever, sunlight fills the room.

The Angel Talks of Beethoven's Genius

By Angela Liu

THE FIRST time the angel sleeps with me, I ask what kind of music God likes to listen to.

He tells me Heaven's got Chopin's *Preludes* blaring all day, trilling arpeggios from invisible hands, but God's real partial to *Ode to Joy*. He thinks Beethoven just gets him, that sometimes a person just needs to lose something important to see what really matters.

The angel's body is bright, like staring at the sun during a bad hangover—it's a high you're not sure is divination or just extreme oxygen-deprivation. Either way, he lectures me about classical music as he moves above me. Did I know that Beethoven used to keep a rod in his mouth, pressing the metal to the piano so he could hear

the vibration of the strings even after his ears
had given out? That Beethoven lost his hearing
and learned to listen to the songs of angels?

I don't answer. We're not on a first-name ba-
sis. I don't even know what to call him, to be
honest. Do angels have names or does God just
assign them numbers like barcoded library
books he lends out to humans? Or is it more
like a word human throats and tongues simply
can't curve around?

The angel doesn't last very long; he says it's
been a while.

"I needed that," he says, laying his head down
on my lap.

I can't tell if he's crying. He's facing away
from me, toward the old television, the one my
cousin let me have when she moved out to Sili-
con Valley for a new start-up stint. His shoulders are quivering, so I stroke his hair as if com-
forting a small child that's just seen a nightmare.

"I'll return the favor," he says defensively. "I
always do."

"It's okay," I say, running a hand over his
forehead, over the cold sweat.

"It's hard too, you know, always listening to
people's problems and not being able to do anything about it," he says.

"I know, I know," I say, my fingers running
over the bump on his back where his wings re-
tracted before he'd undressed. It looks like the
fleshy scar under my mother's navel, the one
perfectly covered by the top of her threadbare

underwear that I used to stare at as a kid when we took our bath together. "Right here," she used to say, making a gentle slicing motion. "This is where the doctor pulled you from me." Before that life-giving cord connecting us almost suffocated me.

"God never tells us his big plan either," the angel says, flinching at my touch, and I'm suddenly overcome with tenderness. A part of me wonders if I could hurt an angel. If it would feel different than hurting a person. More like wounding a flower or strangling the ocean, the grid of pain on a different plane entirely.

"What did you do before you were an angel?" I ask, looking at his warped reflection in the television screen.

He sits up and tells me it's forbidden to talk about an angel's past, like opening up a classified patient record at a hospital. He is terminally chained to God.

Still, he doesn't want to lose a chance to talk. It's not all the time that someone asks about him instead of his boss.

"My mom used to make me play piano for like six hours a day," he says. "She'd scream at me until every note was perfect. Until the tips of my fingers were raw, and I could hear the music everywhere—in the bathroom, in stairwells, even in bed when I touched myself." The angel picks at a fingernail. "So now every time the big guy puts Beethoven on, I feel kind of sick. But like a good kind of sick, you know? Like maybe it's healing me in a way."

It's funny, I think. How even an angel needs to come up with excuses for why its body deserves the suffering it endures.

"Have you ever thought of quitting?" I ask.

He doesn't answer, but I feel the bump on his back twitch under my fingers.

An angel is anointed by God. The VIP-only room in heaven, the chosen squeezing inside like moths hungry for divine light.

He tells me of how Beethoven spent his whole life falling in love. How he named more than a dozen musical pieces after different women, more enamored with each than the last. You can spend a whole lifetime like that, he tells me, falling in and out of love, dedicating yourself to someone else, searching for a mouth that will let you call it home.

I don't tell him how some moths are born without mouths, living no more than a few nights, just long enough to scramble for a mate, to fulfill their evolutionary responsibility and then die alone.

"Beethoven impressed Mozart with improvisation. A stroke of genius. But Mozart never saw the thousands of hours Beethoven diligently practiced with his father so that he could improvise so brilliantly," the angel continues. "True genius cannot shine without discipline. God always mentions this when he comes to check up on us."

I want to tell the angel that Beethoven died in

1827 of a bad liver, bedridden and depressed. How not even the trilling song of angels could rouse his corpse.

"Does He ever check up on the humans?" I ask.

"Of course not. That's what us angels are for," he tells me, smirking like I've finally hit the point he's come here for. "We're here to show you God's good will."

My mother used to say good will is always ninety-nine percent intention and one percent action. She used to work sixteen-hour days ironing strangers' clothes until she burned her hands so badly with the industrial steamer that she thought she was dying.

"For just a moment," she used to say, "I thought I saw heaven."

"God shows his love through trials," the angel tells me. Hadn't I ever read about Herakles and his trek into hell?

I nod, imagining Beethoven with the metal rod between his lips, hearing the music through his mouth instead of the hollow of his ears. How he must have searched the vibrations for meaning, like a satellite scanning the night sky for a signal. You can spend your whole life that way—searching for meaning.

Contributors

RUTH CROSSMAN ("Reptilia") is a community educator and Pushcart-nominated author. Her work has appeared in publications including *sPARKLE&bLINK*, *MaximumRocknRoll* and *Litro*. ruthcrossman.com

HEATHER SAGER ("I Will Work For Love") lives in Illinois, where she writes poetry and fiction. Most recently, her work has appeared in *Poetry Pacific*, *The Bluebird Word*, *Setu*, and other wonderful places.

JAMIE HITTMAN ("The Incredible Exploding Woman") received her MFA in creative writing from Queens College and her medical degree from the University of Maryland. Find her on Twitter: @nimbustiel.

ELIZABETH STIX's debut short-fiction collection, *Things I Want Back From You*, published by Black Lawrence Press in 2024, includes (under a slightly different title) her memorable Fabulist tale "Gustavo and Emiline."

PATRICIA FLAHERTY PAGAN ("Mystery of my Yearning for You, Winged One") is the award-winning author of "Trail Ways Pilgrims" and "Enduring Spirit: Stories." She is also a developmental editor and sensitivity reader.

JENNY BITNER ("The Answerer") has been published in *Mississippi Review*, *The Sun*, *Fence*, and *Best American Nonrequired Reading*. Her novel *Here Is A Game We Could*

Play was published in 2021 from Acre Books.

MARGUERITE HOGAN ("You Can Take It From Here") is a lawyer, writer, yogini, and rookie pole dancer based in Brooklyn and Asheville, North Carolina. Her writing appears in *The Great Smokies Review* and *Kakalak 2021*.

CLAIRE ANDERSON ("Your Invisible Neighbor") is a writer, and an art and film historian from Houston. Her poems have appeared in *Alchemy* and *The Decadent Review*, among other publications.

ENYA MAYNE is a Psychology PhD student, an artist, and an all-around weirdo. Between the novels she reads, the words she jots down, and the drawings she creates, ink is what sustains her. She lives in Ontario.

LOREN RHOADS ("Protection Spell") is the author of *222 Cemeteries to See Before You Die*, *Morbid Curiosity Cures the Blues*, and the short-story collection *Unsafe Words*. lorenrhoads.com

VERONICA MONTES is the author of the chapbooks *Waiting* (Black Lawrence Press) and *I'm Not Lost* (Ethel), as well as *Benedicta Takes Wing*, a collection of short fiction (Philippine American Literary House).

JOE BELARGE ("Rendezvous at the Pier") is a physicist, a chess enthusiast, and a poor but aspiring drummer. Above all else, he enjoys spending time with his family, and he is grateful for their support of his writing habit.

JYOTSNA SREENIVASAN ("Phase") is the author of *These Americans* and *And Laughter Fell From the Sky*. She was a finalist for the PEN/Bellwether Prize. She was born and raised in Ohio. jyotsnasreenivasan.com

BRITTANI JENEE' CAL ("Supernova") is a multiracial writer and poet. Her work has been published in *Page Turner Magazine* and *The Fairy Tale Magazine*. She enjoys forest bathing, birdwatching, and stargazing.

LIAM HOGAN has stories in *Best of British Science Fiction* and in *Best of British Fantasy*, *Analog*, *Daily Science Fiction*, and *Flame Tree Press*, among others. happyendingnotguaranteed.blogspot.co.uk

MEG POKRASS ("A New Pair of Lips") is the author of eight flash fiction collections. Her work has appeared in *The Best Small Fictions 2022* and the *Wigleaf Top 50 2022*. She is the series co-editor of *Best Microfiction*.

Writing by JEFF FRIEDMAN ("A New Pair of Lips") has appeared in *American Poetry Review*, *Poetry*, *Poetry International*, and many others. He has received an NEA Literature Translation Fellowship and numerous other awards.

KATIE KENT ("Mine Again") likes to write stories, mostly YA, about LGTBQ characters, mental illness, and time travel. Her fiction has been published in *Youth Imagination* and *Northern Gravy*, amongst others. katiekentwriter.com.

ALETHEA EASON is the author of the novels *Whispers of the Old Ones* and *Charlotte and the Demons*. Find out more about Alethea in her interview with *Canvas Rebel Magazine*: canvasrebel.com/meet-alethea-eason.

ANGELA LIU ("The Angel Talks of Beethoven's Genius") is a Chinese-American writer/poet, a Nebula finalist, and a 2x Pushcart and Rhysling nominee: liu-angela.com or on Twitter/Instagram @liu_angela